About the author

This is the first adult book the author has written. She is from a large family in Essex. She has two wonderful grandchildren.

The book is partially based on true experiences throughout the author's life.

BE CAREFUL WHAT YOU WISH FOR

Amie Rasar

BE CAREFUL WHAT YOU WISH FOR

Vanguard Press

A CIP catalogue record for this title is
available from the British Library.

ISBN 978-1-784655-72-3

*Vanguard Press is an imprint of
Pegasus Elliot MacKenzie Publishers Ltd.*
www.pegasuspublishers.com

First Published in 2019

**Vanguard Press
Sheraton House Castle Park
Cambridge England**
Printed & Bound in Great Britain

Dedication

To my late sister, Janet.
Loved by everyone,
missed so, so very much

Chapter One

After finishing a long day at work, I headed home. It would have been like any other ordinary day after work, a month previously, but this was the first night I had come home from work and my wife was not home to greet me.

As I put my key in the lock of the front door, I entered my house, the house was cold, unwelcoming and uninviting, there would be no dinner on the table, the dog wouldn't jump up to greet me, I would not bend down to pat him, he would not wag his tail, he would not lick my hand. My wife was not there to throw her arms around my neck and give me a long, lingering, tongue to tongue, warm kiss. I would not feel the stiffening between my legs as she kissed me. The kids would not be shouting, "Daddy, Daddy." The youngest would not be pulling at my trousers for my attention. I wish things were different, I wish I could go back in time, I wish I was there with them but I was not. I wish I had not won the lottery. Be careful what you wish for.

A month previously, we had won over three million pounds on the lottery. We should have been happy, we should have been on a fabulous holiday, the world should have been our oyster, it no longer was. I wanted my old life back, I wanted my kids, I wanted my wife, I wanted my old life, despite our hard times, I would have given all the money back. I wanted my wife and kids back and would do everything and anything to have them back with me. Deep down, I knew they would not come back and my heart ached, I could barely function but I had to carry on. Every day and night I just existed now and never lived. I ached. Oh, how I ached!

Chapter Two

Before the lottery win, we were a happy family, we were a perfect family, that changed the minute that my wife and kids left me. My world fell apart. It would never be the same again.

If only I did not wish to win the lottery…

My mind now etched, and the words engraved on my heart like a tattoo will always be the saying, "Be careful what you wish for."

Chapter Three

I had met my wife when we were both very young. She was a twin and from a large family. I was also a twin, but had not grown up with my brother as we were both put up for adoption, and separated into two different families. My birth parents were both very young when they met and they had to give us away as they could not afford to feed us, let alone clothe us, my brother and I got split up, and to this day, I have never seen my brother again. I often wondered about him, how he was, hoping he was part of a nice family and had nice things, but I would never ever find out unless I searched, and something in me did not want to at this stage, perhaps later in life I would search for him. But at present, I was afraid to, I was scared of the heartache it may bring. I was scared to wish for anything any more.

Chapter Four

On and off over the years, I searched to find my
birth mother and father. I learnt that my mother
and father separated soon after they gave us up,
my mother could not cope and apparently had a
mental breakdown, shortly after giving us away.
She was sectioned and put in a mental home but
instead of helping her it made her worse. She was
in and out of mental homes all her life. Many times
being sectioned, after trying to take her own life. I
learned she had three failed attempts, I knew that
she had tried to take an overdose, then she had
jumped in front of a bus, and then she attempted
to slash her wrist, missing the main artery by two
millimetres. Her health never got any better, only
worse.

She felt like a failed mother and could never live
with the fact she had to give up my brother and I,

she was never the same again. I, personally, did not hold anything against her. I knew at the time she thought she was doing what she thought best and trying to give us the best chance in life.

Little was really known about mental health and treatment back then in the sixties, today, for me in my opinion, the treatments available were nothing short of torture. My mother was given electric shock treatment. It was the early stages for testing the electric shock treatment. Can you imagine, being strapped down having some contraction placed on your head, feeding electricity into the brain, the doctors and specialist believing this sort of treatment will work? Perhaps it did for some, but, in my mind, I feel this sort of thing is best to test on prisoners, like the child molesters, the rapists, the murderers. Test this bloody, so-called, treatment on them before you give it to an innocent young lady that could not get over giving her children away because she could not afford to keep them. Test this on them.

The pain my mother must have endured when they done this to her is hard for me to think about and I know I could never change this for her, I cried for her. I still cry now when I think about her. Still today, I think about her strapped down and given the electric shock treatment, did it work for her? No, it made her worse and she never fully recovered. I think this was the start of her suicide attempts. It really did make her worse, it did not make her better or help her.

I never got over my mother going into a mental institute, it played on my mind day and night, I thought she needed love and cuddles and support of family, not locked up with strangers making strange noises, some unable to talk, some fighting, some even playing with themselves and trying to have sex with each other, unconsented. My mother being touched in her private parts unable to complain as no one took her seriously, blaming her mental state, all washed under the carpet. No one, not one member of staff blinking an eyelid, like it was normal, some patients laying in their bed on the verge of unconsciousness where they have been drugged up. In some rooms the handles were taken off the doors to stop patients getting out, did this really help them? I think not, it made them worse.

I started to research about mental and psychiatric hospitals and now, in 2018, if you go on to the internet you can do a virtual visit. Even going on these sites today freaks me out. I cry for the patients. I cry for their families. It really upsets me what they must have gone through.

Today, treatment has come a long way, and it is not the same treatment as they did in the sixties. Thank God.

One hospital in particular, that is now closed down, that I live near, in mile end, that was called St. Clements, they have recently built this into lovely apartments, but there is still a tower from the old hospital visible from the road. It really makes my skin crawl looking up at it and it gives me the 'heebie jeebies' as my Irish mother would say, I still do not know what this means, 'heebie jeebies.', I guess the equivalent most would say today – "that scared the shit out of me" but when I look up at the tower, I can see a girl hanging from the inside, she has taken her own life, I don't know if it is in my mind or what I think I can see but it scares the fuck out of me. I see a young female with dark hair, her head hanging to the left. She is wearing a blue, long sleeved top and a white type of apron dress, I am not sure if she is a patient or member of staff, but she is still, very still and just hanging from the bell in the tower.

As I pass I say to myself, "Don't look up." I repeat in mind, but I do – in my mind I need to know if I see her every time. Did I imagine it or is it my mind playing tricks on me thinking about my mother? So I look up nearly every day, sometimes the young girl is there, sometimes not. On the days she is there, I go to work and spend most of the time thinking about her. Hoping she was not tortured, and hoping she is now at peace. It makes me sad. It was only when I reached work one particular day, I had an overwhelming urge to look up the hospital on the internet.

I discovered that the St. Clements hospital was once a psychiatric hospital. That really freaked me out.

Oranges and Lemons nursery rhyme would never be sung in my home to my children. The nursery rhyme reminded me of the people that had once been in the hospital and the memories of my mother always came flooding back to me to haunt and upset me. I just wanted to block these memories from my thoughts. I put the thoughts of my mother to the back of mind and tried to get on and lead a normal, happy life.

Over the years, I tried to find as much information as I could about my birth parents. I knew they were both alive and I did not want to cause my mother further heartache, or any relapse so I thought I would track down my father first. And perhaps I would search for my mother later in life. When I knew in my heart it would be the right time, the best time. But I thought it was for the best not to trace her at this stage, I did not want to hurt her or have the memories come flooding back to her and cause her to self-harm again or have any more attempts at taking her life. I did not want her to relapse. It was this that cemented my decision to search for my father first.

Chapter Five

The Search

My search for my birth father now began. It was a lot harder than I first thought. It took almost three years to track down my father and after hard work and many traces, I eventually found a very promising lead.

I discovered that my father could not bear his life and all the memories after giving my brother and I up and he hated everything around him, his home, his friends, his work.

Day to day living for my father became impossible and eventually he moved to a different country, thinking the past would somehow be wiped from his memory and a new life for him would begin without the memories of his past. He thought moving to a completely different country and starting over again on his own would be best for him.

After years of searching, I finally tracked him down to Australia. I wanted answers, I wanted to know everything, I wanted to see my mother, I wanted my father to tell me what happened, where she was. I wanted them to tell me where my twin was. I wanted them to hug me, I wanted them to tell me they loved me, I wanted them to show me that, they too, had been searching for me, I wanted proof they missed me. There was a piece of me missing and I wanted it back. I felt like a jigsaw with a missing piece. I just wanted that one piece to make me complete.

I now had an address, and with his address in one hand and a packet of tissues in the other, I was crying and could not stop, I was not sure if I was extremely happy or extremely frightened and scared. Whatever it was I was feeling, I was on my way to have the answers I longed for all my life.

Chapter Six

I saved hard, sometimes going without food, walking to work part of the way, putting a little bit of money aside and at last, I finally had enough money to do the journey.

I booked a flight and I flew out to Australia in the summer of 2017. I arrived at the airport and looked around, it was wonderful. Everywhere looked so clean. The air was fresh, the people all looked clean and smartly dressed. It was a different world, a far cry from where I just came from, no wonder my father chose to settle down here, I thought.

I put my hand in my jacket pocket and pulled out an A4 piece of paper that had been folded twice. Outside the airport there was a neat line of taxis with the drivers standing outside their cars waiting for passengers to take a ride.

I unfolded the paper and looked at the address, I headed towards the line of taxis, I approached the first one and I went to speak, I tried to say my father's address my mouth opened but there was no speech. The driver looked at me.

"Are you OK, sir?" He said.

I nodded and showed him the sheet of paper with my father's address on it.

"You would like to go there?" he said, pointing at the writing on the paper. "Nice area, very nice. You staying there, sir? You on vacation?" he said.

All I could do was nod. He opened the boot of the car and placed my small suitcase inside.

He then opened the back door of the taxi. I climbed inside. The seats were of cream colour and made of leather. I sat in silence. Staring out of the window going over and over what I was going to say when I reached my destination. I was frightened. I was scared. I was shitting myself. I flew halfway around the world, waited for this moment all my life and today I was going to meet my father. Secretly, I could not wait, my heart was beating fast, I wondered what he looked like, I wondered what colour of hair he had, I wondered what he smelt like, I wondered what he would be wearing. I wondered if he would say 'Good day' or would he greet me like I would greet him if we met in

London and just say 'hi' or 'hello' and reach out a hand for a handshake? Would he recognise me? Would he hold out his two strong arms and pull me into his chest and cry, 'Son'? Would he cry like I have for him? All this was going around and around in my head. Today, at last, I would be with my father.

Chapter Seven

I came out of my thoughts as I heard the driver say something.

I could hear the driver speaking but I was not really hearing what he was saying to me. I was still thinking of what I was going to say when I reached my father's home.

I was suddenly aware that the car had stopped.

"Sir, sir, we have reached your destination," the driver said.

I stared out of the window at the house at which we arrived.

The driver got out of the vehicle and went to the boot pulling my little case from it. He then opened my door.

"G'day, sir, enjoy your stay," the driver said. Then handed my case to me.

I passed him the fare in Australian dollars, nodded at him and managed to say thank you.

In my left hand I still had the A4 piece of paper with my father's address on it along with some of my personal documentation from the airport.

I stood outside for what seemed hours, in reality it was more like minutes.

It was a very large home with a garage. A front garden that was half the size of a tennis court. A far cry from what he and my mother had in England.

I gathered the strength to start the walk to the front door, my heart pounding from my chest, my heart felt like it was jumping out from my chest, I felt like I could grab it. I felt numb, I felt sick, my legs wobbling, my bottom lip trembling, here goes.

I started the walk up the path towards the front door, I reached out my arm, my hand shaking uncontrollably. I grabbed the large silver lion's head knocker. Bang, bang, bang, it seemed so loud and echoed around my head, everything else seemed to have stood still, everything seemed so quiet and all I could hear was the echoing of my knock.

I knocked on the door a fourth time and just as I did the door was answered by a middle- aged woman. She was plump, very pretty and dressed very clean and smart, and was softy spoken. As well as my trembling hand, I was now shaking head to toe. I was still holding the documents in my hand with my father's details on.

"Hi," I managed to say from my dried up mouth, my tongue feeling like leather. I swallowed allowing me to speak further, "Is this the home for Mr AJ Kemp?" I asked.

She stared at me, gave me a smile back and asked who I was. I don't know why but I lied, I am here to deliver some documents.

"Oh," she said "Are you from the coroner's office? Please come in."

My heart was now racing. Coroner's? coroner's… the name coroner's now spinning through my head, I was feeling sick.

"AJ was such a lovely man, I am pleased he did not suffer, such a nice way to go in your sleep, don't you think?" she said in a calm, soft voice.

Chapter Eight

My whole world came crashing down, my life turned upside down in seconds. I felt dizzy, it went dark and I collapsed. I had just discovered my father had passed away the night before.

I came round to find myself on a grey material, very comfortable cushioned chair, the plump female standing over me with a glass of water in her hand.

"Hi," she said, "It must be the heat, you collapsed and we brought you inside. Here, drink this, you will feel better." She handed me the glass.

I took a sip of the water and stared at her. "You said I must be from the coroners. I am not, I am his son."

I wanted to shout, scream, cry, punch, kick but numbness and shock took over and I did nothing. I just sat and stared.

I stared into space, the plump lady stared back, tears trickling down her cheeks. "You're AJ's son? The other twin?" She said.

"You knew he had twins? He told you about us?" I managed to say.

"Of course. When he came out to Australia, he appeared confident and happy, but beyond that I could see there was always something in your father's eyes that was filled with sadness. AJ never talked about it until recently when he became ill, that's when he told me about you and your brother and your mother. He always knew in his heart that you would come to Australia and find him and I gave my promise to him if you turned up that I would hand you a package that he wanted you to have," she said.

She then opened the cupboard next to my chair, pulled a sealed package from it and handed it to me.

"His dying wish was for you to find him, he knew you would come, he always felt in his heart you would come here. He did not go into great detail, all I know is that he carried a lot of heartache as every time he spoke about you and your mother and brother, he broke down. He cried and cried his heart ached when he spoke about you all, I never pushed him to tell me, he used to spend hours on his own with packages, I only assume inside it, is all about your past. I never questioned him about the packages but I made a promise they will get to you no matter what, if you did not come to Australia, I would have come to England to search for you, to track you down. I promised your father they would be delivered. I promised him I would find you, no matter what.

"I do not know what is in this package but he insisted you must have it. There was also one for your brother and mother. Your brother collected his last week but I have your mother's safe."

"My brother was here?" I said.

She nodded back.

I did not ask any more questions, I knew I would be back and maybe would ask then. For now, I could take no more. I ached in every bone. I hurt beyond what anyone knew. I felt sick, numb and like my heart had been ripped out, I wanted the pain to go. I desperately wanted to feel better. My body felt like it was made of lead, I was unable to move. I was unable to function.

Chapter Nine

My Father

As I sat in the chair she placed me in, I just stared, I could not think, I could not move, I could not speak.

I heard nothing when suddenly I heard her voice.

"Your father is still in his bed he passed away in his sleep, we are waiting for the coroner. I know it's a lot for you to take in but if you wish, you can see him," she said.

I was still feeling numb with shock, I did not really have time to think, I just nodded. I went to stand and my legs buckled from me, I placed my hands on the large wooden engraved arms of the chair and pushed myself to my feet. She lead the way up a spiral staircase, to a long corridor with many doors. She pushed open one of the doors and waited for me to pass her.

"Take as much time as you need, I will be downstairs," she said.

Chapter Ten

I entered the bedroom alone, she pulled the door too behind me, the shutters on the window were closed so it was quite dark, I remember a pungent smell, a smell that you cannot describe. A deathly smell, a smell that got into the back of your throat and no matter what you drunk, it did not go away.

I opened the shutters a little to let a bit of light in. For the first time in years I could see my father. He was lying on his back in a big oak four-poster bed. He was grey. He looked shiny. He had blue and white stripy pyjamas on. His hair was slightly grey and pushed back slightly off his forehead. His features looked pointy. I approached the bed, and took his hand, he was cold to the touch. I did not know what to say. I just stood by the bed, holding his hand.

I looked around the room, on the oak bedside table there was a lovely crystal lamp, alongside the lamp there was a picture of him, he looked very young, there was a lady beside him. I assumed it was my mother, I stared at the picture and thought he was very handsome in his younger years. In the picture my mother was holding a baby, my father was also holding a baby. I could only assume this was my brother and I.

I looked down at my father laying in his bed, he did look peaceful, I had a lump in my throat, my eyes filled with tears, tears trickled down my cheeks. I cried and cried, I was now sobbing. Hysterically sobbing, my shoulders going up and down I could not control them. I could not stop, the tears had started streaming from my eyes, snot from my nose now hanging in mid-air. I could not wipe either away, I did not want to let go of his hand. I stood and cried. There was nothing I could do. For the first time in my life, I told my father I loved him. I bent down, and put my hands around his shoulders and tried to hug him, I sobbed and sobbed, I just wanted him to wake up, I would have done anything.

"Dad I am here," I managed to say, hoping he could hear me.

I wanted him to open his eyes, I wanted him to see me, I knew this was not going to happen but regardless I prayed it would.

I hugged him, I kissed his head and said goodbye.

Chapter Eleven

I pulled myself together before returning downstairs, the plump lady must have heard me coming, she called out to me asking if I was OK. I asked for her phone number so I could keep in contact about the funeral. She said she would call me once everything was sorted. I told her I would return to show my last respects to my father. She handed me a piece of paper with her number on it, I picked up the package and wanted to make a quick exit before I broke down again.

I tucked the package under my arm and have never opened it. I had planned to open it when I, or if I, ever met my brother and mother again, and I would open it in front of them. But for now, I would keep it safe and not open it. I was curious to open it, I hoped it would give me the answers I longed for. But for now, I would wait.

I was in no fit state to take any more information in.

From that day, I did not want to experience hurt like that again. I will never get over that. It still makes me cry to think about it, I got so far tracing my father I was at his door, he was on the inside but asleep, he was asleep forever and I would never get my answers from him. Oh, how I ached.

Life sometimes was fucking cruel. A fucking bitch.

For that reason, I was terrified to search for my twin.

I don't want to experience hurt like that again. Now, what I do in my mind is, I dream what I want his life to be like. I can live with that. I imagine him being happy, and not wanting for anything.

He tracked my father down before me, I hope he got the answers he needed. I was happy for him not to have experienced the hurt and pain that I just experienced.

I decided to return to England.

I was not to know at this point, just several months later, February 2018, I would experience the same sort of pain again.

Chapter Twelve

It was a long flight home. The flight had been slightly delayed but I was glad to be back in England.

It felt nice to be back in England. Although I was in shorts and it was cold. It was also raining. I had left my car at the airport and it took just under two hours to reach my address. I pulled in to the drive and made a dash to the front door. As I turned the key in the door, I felt the drips of water on my legs from my jacket, wet from the rain, my fingers purple from the cold, I entered the house that I once called my home.

My Life, My Past

My wife and I lived in Essex, we had a happy marriage. We did not have much money, I worked six days a week to make ends meet. We made the home comfortable but we never had new furniture. We were always given bits and pieces from friends and family. I always knew that I would win the lottery and dreamt most days what I would spend it on, how it would change my life, how nice it would be to have money and not worry about bills.

There were times when we were totally skint and remembered how as a family, we use to eat a lot of pasta and rice as it was filling but also very bland, but we were eating and we were paying the rent. Don't get me wrong, we were not always totally skint but the kids did not go on any school trips, they did not have any birthday or Christmas presents nor Easter eggs, we just did not have the money. We did not buy sweets and treats, we did not even buy biscuits.

To this day, I don't know whether to laugh or cry about the first time we used the food bank.

I returned home with three full bags of groceries and I was unpacking. There were soft toilet rolls, my word these are a luxury when you don't have money. We used to use newspaper or very cheap toilet rolls that graze your arse when you wipe, and your fingers seem to go through the tissue. There were tins upon tins, cereals, sugar, then, the icing on the cake, I pulled out a packet of chocolate biscuits. My kids saw them as I pulled them out from the third carrier bag, they were in a long, light blue packet from a well-known store. The kids screamed with excitement, you would have thought with their delight I pulled out a free holiday to Disneyland the way they acted.

This is when I decided to laugh and not cry. We had no money but we were happy. We smiled. We laughed. My children were everything.

Chapter Thirteen

The Lottery Win

The time was 7.10 p.m. It was Wednesday. I checked my pockets, went down the sides of the second-hand settee, checked the drawers and cupboards and scrapped up enough money to buy a lottery ticket.

"Come on, kids, give me six numbers."

"One," the youngest shouted, followed by, "thirty."

"Fourteen, three and six," the eldest shouted.

"Hold on, hold on, that's enough." I closed my eyes and hovered the pen over the ticket and dropped it down for the sixth number –there I thought, please let it be me.

I went to the local shop and placed my lottery bet with only three minutes before the closing.

We never ever watched the draws on the lottery but I was compelled to watch to see what numbers come out, I just had a strange feeling.

As I watched number three, fourteen, six, thirty, one… twenty-one…

Oh my God! They were put into order – I had the ticket in my hand, my head kept rolling from my ticket to the television, checking and checking and checking –I had six numbers…

I used to wish and pray that my life changed and also hoped that a lottery win would do just that. My prayers were answered when I had won over three million pounds on the lottery that Wednesday.

Chapter Fourteen

We now had over three million pounds. I had to keep saying it. Three million, three million, I wrote it down, I did not even know how many noughts it was, we were laughing, we were jumping, we were screaming, "Three million! Three million!" The kids were dancing, I was dancing, my wife was dancing.

The youngest, aged four, said, "Daddy, does that mean I can have a sweet now?"

We all looked at each other, it went silent.

I replied, "A sweet? No, darling, not a sweet, it means you can have the whole bloody sweet shop!"

We all hugged, cried and laughed together. We had money – for the first time in our life, we had money. I could buy meat, a leg of lamb, my kids had never seen a leg of lamb, they never tasted a leg of lamb, coke, lemonade, sweets, soft toilet paper for the rest of our lives...What a treat! My God, I could not wait to go to a supermarket and not even look at the price of anything. This was the first thing on my list, we are going food shopping in a normal supermarket, and being able to get a trolley for the first time in years, filling it to the brim. It would feel like heaven. It will feel good. My head would be held high, smiling, smiling again because my kids could eat anything they wanted.

They would also get anything, within reason, that they wanted, I wanted them in my heart to have everything. I wanted to spoil them, I wanted them to have the best and they would, within reason, but I would make sure their feet were still firmly fixed on the ground. You can only do this if you have come from nothing. People that are born into riches would not know or experience this feeling we are going through. They had never had to go without, they would not know what it is to be hungry, not really hungry, to go days without food. And, in a strange way, I was happy that I experienced this as there are more people like me in the world, and less people than the rich and famous 'stuck up their own arse, my shit don't smell' people.

I did not normally swear but having nothing then to over three million in the bank, was a dream, a prayer, a wish. Whatever it was, it came true. Despite my excitement, my prayers were eventually answered.

Was I happy and will it change my life? Of course it bloody would.

When I used to read or hear people state will the win change you and they say no I used to think to myself, *Really? You lying bastards! Of course it will! How couldn't it? Unless of course you aleady have money and you are rich.*

I was not to know that in just three days' time, my family would leave me and I would experience even worse pain and heartache than I did at my father's address.

Chapter Fifteen

I found myself thinking about my own childhood and I felt lucky that now, with my lottery win, my kids did not have to experience what I went through as a child. I was adopted from birth into a large Irish family. My birth parents gave my brother and I away without the authorities knowledge. My parents had seven children, one girl and six boys, we were one of four families on the estate that had a big four bedroom council corner house. But we were very poor.

We had nothing to eat from day to day. Two days could have gone by without anything to eat. We used to eat discarded food and scrape chewing gum from the streets that a person would have spat out hours or even days before without a second thought, popping it into our tiny mouths because we were so hungry. Today, we would have all been put in care if we lived like this, so at least I am grateful to my adopted parents that they managed to keep us together. It must have been very, very hard bringing up seven children. We never got any Christmas, birthday presents or Easter eggs from our parents. In fact, we did not get anything.

As a kid, we got free dinners at school and this was the only time I ate during the week. For me, I dreaded the school holidays as we would go hungry. I must have been the only child in school that was upset at this time. The school dinner at times was gross, but I knew I had to eat it as I was so hungry and there would be jack shit in the cupboards when I returned home from school. I normally opted for chips but they were not always available, there was always Shepherd's pie – it smelt like cat food and it looked like slops. The mash on top was watery and you could just about see a bit of mince here and there amongst the carrots. It smelt dreadful and even today, I cannot bear to look at Shepherd's pie, let alone eat it. We had dinner ladies that walked around the dinner hall making sure you were eating, if they spotted too much left on your plate they would come and spoon-feed you and I am sure, as I was so undernourished, they thought they were doing me a favour by putting more and more on my plate. I use to dread the dinner lady spotting me as I knew she would spoon-feed me. She asked how many sisters and brothers I had, I innocently said six, she would pick up the spoon and scrape the mess before me, which they called Shepherd's pie onto the huge spoon that barely fitted into my mouth, and before every spoon she said what are your brother's and sister's names? I would reply back their names, she would get this mess on the spoon and start repeating the names back to me and put each heap into my mouth.

One for Jamie, one for Joseph, one for Peter, one for John, one for Paul, one for Simon, one for Rosey… she carried on until all my dinner had gone from the plate.

I was no longer hungry but wanted to vomit. In a strange way at weekends when I was home it prevented me from feeling hungry and I was grateful to the dinner lady, as my mind drifted back to her spoon feeding me, and I no longer felt hungry but sick. I no longer wanted any food.

I remember to this day the dinner lady that used to always spot me smelt like liver and bacon, she appeared small for her age, she had wrinkles, she had grey and white curly short hair, probably the equivalent of a blue rinse today, and she wore a blue checked tabard. She paced the dinner hall looking side to side with hands in her pockets. She was nice, don't get me wrong, but I dreaded her seeing me as she used to take it upon her that I liked custard and got me extra and she spooned it in my mouth repeating the same procedure – one for Jamie, one for Joseph. Oh, fuck. I would cry inside, here we go again! When I told her I was full up or I did not like it, she would just seem to ignore me and kept that spoon coming at me. Again, I cannot bear to see or smell custard today as I start heaving. To be honest, I cannot remember anything else on the menu, I'm not too sure they had one, I am going back fifty years or so. School in itself I did like, for poor families like us at school, in winter was a godsend, it was when we were warm, at home, there was no central heating like today.

The families today have it easy, flick of a switch for most household's and you get instant heat, but when I was a child we had one coal fire in the main living room and seven of us had to huddle around it. We cooked on it, and we dried our clothes around it. One of my most favourite memories was huddling around the fire, my father sitting beside us with a huge fork with a wooden handle and a plate of buttered bread. He used to take one slice at a time, put the fork through the bread and toast on one side on the fire, the butter melting and making a hissing sound as it fell into the fire. It would go a golden brown colour on the underneath of the bread, once browned, he then passed it to one of us and we folded it in half whilst still hot and ate it. It was one of the most wonderful things I had ever eaten.

However, some items were also put on the fire to be disposed of. As a kid, I never knew what they were and at the time I did not know our mother used to burn her used sanitary towels on it. I learnt this in later life. I did not have a clue back then when I was a child. I remember as a child when we were ushered out of the living room and my mother would enter the living room and we were not allowed back in until our mother came out. When we went back into the living room the fire was roaring and there were signs of a new burnt item but we did not question it. I now know the sanitary towels were burnt on our open fire, not sure what other mothers or women did with them. I just hoped that we used to have our toast before this event and not after. I cannot remember but it makes me gag when I look back on it. We also used to have a little canary called Joey and my dad use to let him out of his cage and put a bowl of water on the fire guard and a towel and, no word of a lie, he used to jump in the water, have a bath and wipe himself on the towel. How he never flew in the fire I don't know, but that is true. I loved Joey. He was bright yellow and had a brown circle on his head like a crown, he was lovely. Our family liked pets, and I still do today. Every Christmas one of our pet rabbits used to escape and we never found them again. I realised my parents tried to fatten them up all through the year, told us they escaped during the night, unknown to us, we were eating it for our Christmas dinner. Our parents telling us it was turkey. I did think it was strange that we never had any white meat, only always brown, we were eating our pet. This went on for years without any of us realising until I was asked to fetch some coal from the shed one Christmas Eve and saw my favourite rabbit, Bluey, was hanging by its back legs inside. That's when I questioned my parents, they swore to me that Bluey had caught a virus and they hung him in the shed and were going to tell us after Christmas so as not to upset us all.

Every bloody year we ate our pets. I think that's why I have become a doctor Doolittle and will take any pet in today. I think I am trying to make up for eating Bluey and all the Bluey's before him.

We had many pets over the years, but our parents only killed the rabbits to eat. Not sure how we could afford to keep them, but we did. It's strange, no matter how poor you are there is always a pet in the family.

I watch programmes today about poor families, poor people living on benefits and they always have a dog or pet in tow, it was no different back then over fifty years ago.

We had no end of rabbits, the fuckers breed and breed. We thought we had the same sex rabbits and only had one cage, we soon ended up with twenty-six of them. My father made us sell the little ones to the local pet shop.

I remember my brothers and myself carrying them all the way to the local pet shop, when I said local, it was about six or seven miles away, we used to take a short cut through the park, it was called Belhus Park, many years ago. On the way we passed the woods, one time there was a strange man in the woods, he was staring at us with his cock out playing with himself. We were not frightened, we just shouted at him, "put it away, it isn't even big!" Not sure why we had this reaction but he did not faze us. Perhaps it was because on regular occasions we had to make this walk to sell our baby rabbits, and if we showed fear or reported him we would not be allowed to do the journey again, who knows?

Only a few weeks later in the local paper a horse rider going through the woods where we saw the pervert and reported him, now there were police at the gates leading to the park on a regular occasion.

We walked from Kenningtons to a place called South Ockendon, this is where the 'big' shops were, as we used to call them. The pet shop would take them all off us and in return give us just a few pounds. But we were very grateful for the money.

Our parents were happy as we could not keep the baby rabbits as we did not have a hutch for them and we could to not afford to feed them.

I remember vividly being so excited to wake up and go outside to feed them, seeing lots and lots of fur in the hutch, that meant they were preparing a bed for the babies they were about to have. I checked each morning and eventually, it must have been a day or two, there appeared about seven babies. They did not have fur they were so small, warm and pink. I am not sure how long we waited to take the same walk to the pet shop, but I knew I could carry more than one in my hands. I think in the same position today it would break my heart giving baby rabbits away, but back then in my child's mind-set it was what you had to do.

We were even given a macaw one year. But we could not afford a cage and had to give it away. We gave it to a relative, they built an aviary in their garden to keep it in. We handed it over to the new owners and they put it in it, it died the same night.

I was so upset. It must have been too cold for it. As in our home it was in the living room and we had that coal fire, so it went from one extreme to the other so I guess the shock of the coldness killed it. It was a beautiful bird, vivid blue and yellow and so, so big. I have always wanted another macaw.

Chapter Sixteen

After returning from the regular walk from South Ockendon back to our home, we had a few pounds from the pet shop and we were all sat around the fire and we were lucky enough to eat tonight. My Mother would come in with a plate of buttered bread and a huge fork with a wooden handle. My father would then toast it over the coals, passing one slice to each of us, for our tea that night. My brothers, sister and I were grateful for eating that night. If my parents had enough coal they would try and keep it going until we went to bed. Getting from the living room to the bedroom, my God, that was like running the gauntlet, coming out of the living room where it was warm to the rest of the house where it was cold, colder than a fridge but not as cold as a freezer. We would change out of our school uniform then put on our pyjamas that had been held in front of the fire to make them warm then would we run. Run down the long hallway up the stairs, past the bathroom then into the end bedroom where I shared with two brothers and jumped into a freezing bed. We did not have duvets in those days but horrible eiderdowns, nylon stretched sheets that you got stuck to, and feather pillows, the feathers use to stick through the pillow case and dig you in the face. Then I remember my mother putting heavy fur coats on top of us, once these bastard things went on top of you, you could not move they were so heavy so whatever position you were in when Mother chucked them on top, you were like that when you woke. I remember her always going to the church jumble sales bringing back fur coats in the summer and often thought why she needed them; it was not until the winter I found out. They also smelt very dusty.

I remember my father growing potatoes in the back yard if they were in season, we were lucky we would get chips but they were cooked in the most disgusting lard or dripping that had been in a roasting dish in the kitchen for Christ knows how long.

I came from a large family and things were tight. The only time we ever got a new piece of clothing was from the school board. Years ago, poor families like us would be given a voucher, which entitled us to get a school uniform once a year. And yes, only once, so if you grew quick you were out of luck. My sister was lucky as she wore skirts so my Mother would get them a little longer so she grew into them. She would to have to turn the waist band over to make it the right length, then as she got taller, unravel the waist band so the skirt got longer as she got taller.

I, on the other hand, had to have trousers so you can imagine I ended up wearing my trousers and by the second term they were 'jack ups' and I could have worn them as shorts. I was bullied. Today, I have managed to buy my children what they need and they don't have to go through what I went through.

So when we got this voucher we had to go to a shopping centre, this is the only time we visited the shop, at any other time, my parents would not be able to afford anything inside. It was one of the main stores that is still open today. We entered the lift and the school shop was on the third floor there was not a lot of choice especially the shoes, oh my God, the shoes they were the worst of the worst, they were horrid. There was only one style – they never, ever changed. I had the same style of shoes all through juniors and seniors and the bastard things never ever wore out, so even if my parents were able to afford a new pair, I wouldn't need them. And heavy, you could not run in them they were so heavy. Then I noticed the only difference between mine and sisters shoes were the laces. They were the same style. They were horrid, again I had new shoes but I was bullied for them, as the uniform and shoes no other bloody shop sold them so everyone knew not only that you were poor, but you also got a voucher for your uniform and where you got the hideous clothes from.

Chapter Seventeen

Alone My Family Left Me

The lottery win had changed my life, all this money – my family left me, why did I ever wish?

As the days, weeks, months went by I was coping with living alone, it was still hard coming through the front door after work with no one to greet me. I knew I would never accept it but I was beginning to live with it, if only I could turn the clock back.

But I couldn't.

Now, my life changed and all I had was memories. I would now come home from work not physically tired any more but more mentally, it was torture but I knew I had to accept my wife and children had all left me.

I would go into the kitchen and switch the kettle on, open the fridge only to find a little milk, butter and a half slab of cheese that was dark around the edges and sporting mould around the edges. *I must get on top of all this*, I thought to myself. I will do shopping monthly, enough to last, like my wife had done before for me and the kids. I looked in the freezer – a frozen piece of trout stared back at me, it had that stare like it had just been hooked, its eyes opened wide. I opened another drawer in the freezer but there was nothing much more to eat. Beans on toast it will have to be until I get shopping at the weekend.

I picked the can of beans from the shelf in the cupboard and stared at the bluey green label. Squeezing the tin, I remembered my wife, I remembered the good times, I was now so lonely, I slumped to the floor with my head between my knees and sobbed.

I cried until I ached, snot was now hanging from my nostrils, tears rolling down my cheeks, the tears hitting the lino bounced and dispersed as they hit the floor. I must have closed my eyes and started to dream.

I was laying in the bath, bubbles surrounded me, the jets of water hammering against my skin, the bath tub was large enough to accommodate both of us. The water was neck level, my legs stretched out and my relaxed cock bobbing on the water. My wife was standing at the side of the bath, she started to undress and as she unzipped her dress, it fell to the black marble, silver speckled floor. She was standing in her black lacy bra, silky knickers and stockings. My penis began to grow, it was now fully erect and standing out of the water. My wife turned around with her back to me, she bent over and stood close enough to the bath so I could reach at her. I pulled at her black silky knickers pulling them down to her knees, between her legs she was very warm and wet and smelt delicious. I began to caress her buttocks with one hand, with the other hand I slid my fingers in her, she felt and smelt so good. She made a quiet groan, I slid my fingers in and out faster and faster, I started to lick at her, I licked around her buttocks then spun her around, all the time she was groaning louder and louder, then all off a sudden I woke.

I opened my eyes in disbelief. I was on the kitchen floor, I was not in the bathroom like moments before. It was a vivid dream. It made me think it was real, it made me think my wife was by my side. I sat and stared at the bean tin then threw it at the wall, I cried, it hurt. I missed my wife. I missed my children. I missed my life.

I had these sort of dreams often, they were nice when they were happening to me, but so hurtful and heart wrenching when I woke. But I did not want them to stop.

I also dreamt about the kids, these would be very happy dreams, although we had no money we were happy. The trips to the park, the feeding the ducks , the walks in the woods, they did not cost anything but as a family it was the best you could get.

My thoughts drifted back to the park, my kids sitting on the swings and I was behind them pushing them in turn, my wife sitting in front on a bench with the sun beaming down, the children really enjoying themselves, their little legs going back and forth trying to get higher and higher on the swing. I enjoyed life. I enjoyed my family, I love them so much, and I now hated her for leaving me. It was unfair what had I done? Why did I deserve now to be so unhappy, life was such a bitch.

I had to pull myself together, I did not want to curl up and die. I had to fight, to get back to normality.

Chapter Eighteen

Return to Work

It was the start of another week, I returned to work. I was back in the office, everyone being so kind to me, even the people I did not like were pleasant to me, smiling at me, before, they did not even acknowledge me. I found it hard with these people not just to smile back, but I wanted to cry out, "fuck off with that smile, I did not like you before, why should I like and talk to you now? Just fuck off!" But no, I acknowledged them. I felt I had to. They had not spoken to me before my wife left me but rumours got around the office like dog shit around the sole of your shoe.

There is always one person in the work place that is a cunt. There is also one person that thinks they own the place, yet you cannot say anything as you get the blame for bullying. Well, actually, in my office today, the way I felt – they were all cunts. I did not have time for any of them. Yet I found myself having to be politically correct. If you do not know who the cunt is in your office, you are probably the cunt.

Smiling in the right places, waving, saying hello, yet I was aching. I wanted to cry, I did not want to smile. I ached for my wife and children. No one would fully understand until they had been in the same situation. But I would never wish that upon anyone.

Being a man, I felt I was expected just to get on with my life, to harden to the situation. On the outside I could, on the inside I was dead. I ached, I hurt, I could not breathe, I crumbled, I was sad. I had over three million in the bank and yet, I was very, very sad.

Some of my colleagues were actually very nice. I did get on with them, but I would not tell them any of my private life. Don't get me wrong, I used to have conversations like what we did at the weekend when we finished work, but personal stuff I kept to myself. They only found out my wife and children left me because I had to take emergency leave and I had to call in. The staff member that took the call, she was better and quicker than Twitter for gossip – she was a nosey bastard that one. No sooner had I put the phone down telling her that I had to have emergency leave, not only did the whole department know, but the local sandwich shop too. My God, that one used to like a gossip.

In fact, to be honest, her telling everyone did me a favour really as when I did return to work I did not get people approaching me saying, "Hi, I have not seen you for a while, have you been on holiday?" And that sort of comment.

It seemed that people were almost scared to say much more than hello to me.

Chapter Nineteen

Remembering

In the following weeks and months, I felt myself always thinking about my wife and children, they were never negative thoughts, they were always nice. I can honestly say we did not argue, we did not fight, we were each other's rock. That is why I found it so hard to cope, when she left me and took the children with her.

I remember at weekends we would all get ready, no matter what the weather, and if it was raining before heading out my wife would put meat, vegetables and stock in the slow cooker to make a stew ready for our return.

Today it was raining. My wife prepared the stew, peeling the carrots, potatoes and onions then chopping them into bite-sized pieces placing them into the slow cooker with the chunks of meat we managed to get at cost price because the sell-by date was due. Then, making a gravy, she poured this over the contents and put the lid on the slow cooker and switched it on.

She then joined the children and I as we put on our coats and wellies, we would all head off on a walk, not really sure where we were heading, we would just set off and see where our legs took us.

Today, we headed towards the canal, it had been raining and there was a lovely, perfectly arched coloured rainbow in the distance, the colours were so bright and vivid, I told the children to look up and teased them and told them whenever you see a rainbow and it arched over a house the people that lived there would be lucky for life and riches would fall upon them.

On the Wednesday when we won the lottery, it had been raining and there was a bright rainbow that towered above our home, my children saw it and they were convinced I had won because of the rainbow and that made me smile inside and out.

We continued our journey, passing moored narrow boats as people cycled past us. The kids were running a few feet in front of us jumping in every puddle they could find, the mud splashing up their coats and hitting their little red cheeks as they both giggled. They then would run to the next puddle, jumping harder into it than the previous puddle, both of them roared with laughter as a large piece of mud hit the youngest on her head sticking in her lovely blonde locks of hair.

No amount of money could buy this happiness, we were happy, very happy.

How I had the perfect family. How I missed them all so very much.

~

We had now walked the length of canal and decided to head back home, we were all exhausted. I put the youngest on my shoulders, her red, muddy wellies sticking out either side of my face.

We reached home and my wife and children stood on the mat outside the front door pulling off their wellies. As the door opened, we smelt the sweet smell of the stew that was bubbling away in the slow cooker waiting for us when we returned.

The children and my wife went inside as I picked up all the wellies and went around to the back of the house to hose them down, ready for another day.

My children were put in the bath and my wife had washed all the mud from their hair, face and hands. From downstairs I heard the laughter as they played with their toys and bubbles in the bath.

I started to lay the table and serve the hot stew that had been cooking ready for our return.

The children came running down the stairs in their pyjamas ready for their tea and we sat around the table all talking and laughing about the day's events. The children kept asking about the rainbow and was it really true that if the rainbow went over anyone's house they would be lucky.

I said, "Of course it's true, and one day they may find out if it ever went over our house." That Wednesday, when I won the lottery, they never asked about the rainbow again, they totally believed the story I told them. Bless them.

The children finished their tea and I took them upstairs to bed, tucked them both in and started to read their favourite books: *Mr Stewpot* and *ABC, Explore the Garden with Me*. The ABC books they adored, they loved learning about insects and animals, they loved the characters from the books.

They seemed to fall asleep in the same place in the book, the books taught the children the alphabet along with all different fruits and vegetables and interesting facts about insects and animals. As soon as we reached the letter 'M' for 'mango', they were sound asleep. They looked so peaceful, calm and happy. I often wondered if they carried on the story in their little heads. After turning the children's light off and pulling the door too, I went downstairs.

Chapter Twenty

Our Time

My wife and I now found our time. Sometimes we would just chill out in front of the television, sometimes we would play music or a board game, but, no matter what we did, we would also have a lovely bottle of red wine or two.

At times we would just sit in a quiet room, no television, no sound from music, and chat – chat about nothing really, just pouring red wine. It was on these nights my wife would disappear upstairs, I thought, to check on the children, but no, she was getting dressed up. She would call me upstairs and I would go rushing up to find her on the bed wanting me.

As I entered the bedroom, there in front of me, staring back was my wife, kneeling on the bed, her bum up in the air. I could just see the back entry of her lovely precious covered in dark, curly hair. She looked wet, I could see her hand, she was playing with herself telling me to join her.

I pulled off my shirt, down came my trousers and before me my hard, stiff cock was ready to roger.

As I knelt behind her and slumped over her back, grabbing at her breast, my cock touching the end of her backside. She was moaning and groaning, she twisted her hands behind her and grabbed at my cock. Pulling back and forth. God, I found it hard not come in an instant, but I held off, she span around and put my hard weapon inside her mouth, all the time going up and down with her hands. She pulled it out, my juices from my cock were clear as she wiped them all around her face then put my weapon inside her mouth again. We were both groaning as she sucked and sucked until I was almost ready to come then she took me out of her mouth and put me in between her legs. She was wet, warm and so welcoming I thought my cock was going to explode. In and out, my God I wanted to fuck her hard, I felt I could have broken her in two. She felt so nice, every time I fucked my wife it just got better and better, I did not want this moment to end. I could not stop myself. From inside my weapon, my blood was over boiling point, there was an explosion like never before – white cum shooting and shooting. With every shot there was a groan and a kiss from my wife. She pulled me on top of her and cuddled me, her fingernails sunk into my back. She loved me just lying there with my cock inside her. She loved it until my weapon softened and just withdrew from her naturally. She loved it sliding down the crack of her backside. She said it was a lovely feeling having a wet, warm cock glide over her bum. We then fell asleep in each other's arms.

Chapter Twenty-one

The alarm clock was sounding. Fuck! It felt I had no sleep. I turned to my wife, ready to kiss her good morning, I looked down then realised I must have played with myself whilst asleep. I was sticky with cum, my legs and the top sheet were wet. In a split second, I then realised I was dreaming. I grabbed the empty pillow beside me, put it to my face and cried and cried until I could not cry any more.

I had to pull myself together.

Chapter Twenty-two

I had a shower and went to work, trying to concentrate on work related matters, putting my dream into the back of my head.

Work did get easier over the months, at first it was very hard to get back into the routine. The people were generally nice and for the first time I felt that I was getting back to normal.

It was mainly when I was alone that I had my day dreams. I looked forward to having them but at the same time when I woke from them I was very upset. I just wanted my life back, I wanted my wife. I wanted my kids.

Chapter Twenty- three

It was Saturday. I felt lonely. There was no work today. I woke quite late at nine thirty a.m. I used to be up at five a.m. for work so today was a lie in. A long lie in.

I went into the shower and stood there for what seemed ages just letting the water go over my head, running down my stomach. I felt myself thinking about my lovely wife. I saw her watching the shower. She was outside the shower and she dropped her silky dressing gown to the floor, she was naked. She opened the door of the shower as I felt my cock stiffen. The water from the shower was now bouncing off my long length. My wife grabbed it, pulling it back and forth, she knew I was ready to explode. She turned around so her back was to me and guided me into her from behind, she moved back and forth. The shower, now steamed up with not just the hot water but our breath, water bouncing off her back as she went back and forth, her breasts knocking against the glass screen, removing the condensation and making two round, perfect circles to see through. My God, it felt good. I tried to my hardest not to cum, but within minutes I exploded inside her.

I realised that I had been wanking myself off whilst thinking about my wife. I continued to shower, washing the sticky cum from my body, it was everywhere, it seemed to stick like glue to the shower. I cleaned it off and turned off the shower.

Today was such an important day.

I spent ages thinking about what to wear.

What did my wife like me best in? I wanted to wear this today. Today was a special but a very horrible day.

I decided to put on my light blue, designer shirt and dark jeans – my wife always said that the blue matched my eyes. Yes, this was a good choice.

I dressed and got in to the car to start my journey.

Chapter Twenty-four

I felt very nervous, I had flashbacks from the lottery win.

I was back in that Wednesday night.

I called Camelot, they had arranged for us to go to headquarters to pick up our winnings.

We travelled to Camelot in separate cars, as my wife had a meeting with the school in the morning and she said she would meet me at Camelot with the children.

We met at headquarters at three p.m. on the Friday of the same week.

We were all signed in by Camelot, there are very strict rules – you cannot even use the toilet without being escorted. They take the ticket from you, it gets checked numerous times, this procedure is a very anxious time but everything goes through your head, you know it's a genuine ticket but you start to feel what if it's not? I know it's a silly thing but you imagine all sorts.

You wait in a room whilst they go off to check the ticket, they finally come back to you and say, "congratulations! You are the winner of Camelot." Then they offer you talks with bank managers, the bank managers are there waiting to give advice. The money gets deposited immediately when you choose your bank.

I think to myself, just give me the money! I want to go to the cash point and get a statement, I want to see what the figures look like. I want to leave it in the machine for the person queuing behind me. I am excited and my wife and kids have beaming smiles. For the first time in my life, I really cannot described the feeling. It feels so, so bloody good.

We pick our bank, it is the same as the Queens, I had never heard of the bank before this day, but it seemed a good choice to us. So, now, we had over three million in the bank. I turned to my wife and children and I told them how much I loved them and how we no longer would want for anything. I hugged and kissed them all. We were happy. We were ecstatic. What a wonderful feeling!

Chapter Twenty-five

We left headquarters and headed back to our cars, my wife took the kids, and I travelled alone.

We agreed to meet at a very posh restaurant to celebrate. Both our immediate families were going to meet there. We were so excited.

I told my wife to follow me – throughout the journey I kept looking in my rear-view mirror waving, they were waving back. I kept blowing them kisses, they all blew kisses back to me. We were all so happy.

I looked in my rear-view mirror ready to wave and blow another kiss – I blew the kiss and went to wave and I saw a lorry coming too fast at my wife's car – a shriek and a bang, in slow motion, the lorry hit my wife's car rolling it onto its roof and smashing it into the central reservation. I slammed on my brakes. I couldn't move, my hands seemed glued to the steering wheel. Cars stopping all around me. My door opened as I heard a man's voice asking if I was OK.

I could not answer.

"My wife, my kids…"

"OK, sir. I can call them," he replied back.

"NO, NO, NO! They are in that car," I said, pointing to the upturned car.

They were all killed instantly.

That's how my wife and kids left me.

Be careful what you wish for.